Young Learner's

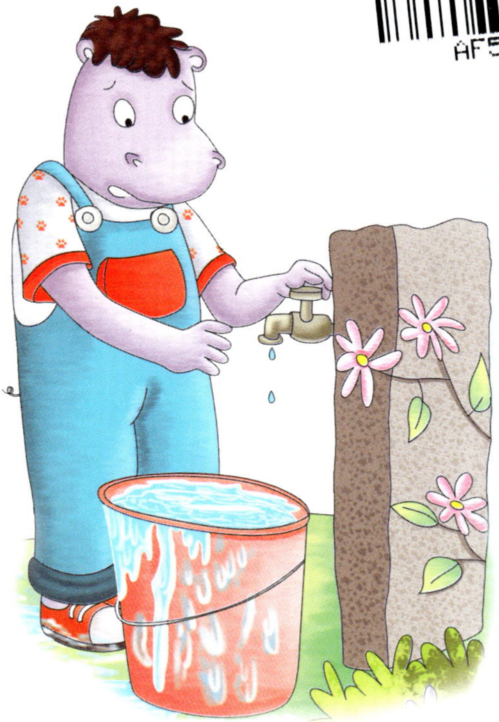

Fufu Saves Water

Sangita Koushik

Fufu was a responsible hippo. He was always careful not to waste anything. Water was one of them.

He made sure that all the taps and pipes in his house worked well and none of them leaked.

Fufu was good friends with his neighbour, Mr. Foxy. One day, Fufu was watering his plants. Suddenly, he heard the sound of water flowing.

He saw that the tap in Mr. Foxy's garden was open. The bucket under the tap had filled up and water was overflowing from it.

Fufu saw Mr. Foxy sleeping in the hammock. Fufu did not want to disturb him, so he went into the garden and turned the tap off.

The next day, he told Mr. Foxy about the overflowing water. Mr. Foxy thanked Fufu. He promised to be careful in the future.

A few days later, Fufu saw Mr. Foxy washing his car. He went over to greet him but his smile vanished. Mr. Foxy was busy washing his car showing no concern about the water being wasted from the open hosepipe.

Fufu went to Mr. Foxy and said, "Mr. Foxy, please turn off the tap. Using hosepipe for washing car wastes a lot of water. You should use a pail for washing your car. It helps in saving water."

Mr. Foxy closed the tap. He laughed and said, "Fufu, you worry too much. It is just water. We have enough water."

Fufu replied seriously, "No, Mr. Foxy! We should not waste water. It is precious! Save every drop as each drop counts."

One day, Fufu went out for some work, and returned late in the evening. He saw Mr. Foxy standing at his gate.

He could see that Mr. Foxy was worried. Fufu asked, "Is everything alright?"

Mr. Foxy replied, "I left the tap open again. Now, the water tank is empty. There is not a single drop of water in my house."

He continued, "I know you have warned me many times. Can I take water from your house?" Mr. Foxy was feeling ashamed of himself.

Fufu smiled and said, "I will give you water only if you promise never to waste it again."

Mr. Foxy replied, "Yes. I have learnt my lesson." And indeed, he had! He never wasted water after that day.

Moral: Use water carefully. It is precious.